BRITAIN IN OLD PHOTOGRAPHS

BELFAST

VIVIENNE POLLOCK &

TREVOR PARKHILL

ULSTER MUSEUM

SUTTON PUBLISHING LIMITED

NATIONAL MUSEUMS & GALLERIES OF NORTHERN IRELAND

Sutton Publishing Limited
Phoenix Mill · Thrupp · Stroud
Gloucestershire · GL5 2BU

Ulster Museum
Botanic Gardens
Belfast BT9 5AB

First published 1997

Reprinted 1999

Cover photographs: front: the small Co-op grocers in
Woodvale Road; back: the almost-finished City Hall.

British Library Cataloguing in Publication Data
A catalogue record for this book is available from the
British Library.

ISBN 0-7509-1754-7

Typeset in 10/12 Perpetua.
Typesetting and origination by
Sutton Publishing Limited.
Printed in Great Britain by
Ebenezer Baylis, Worcester.

CONTENTS

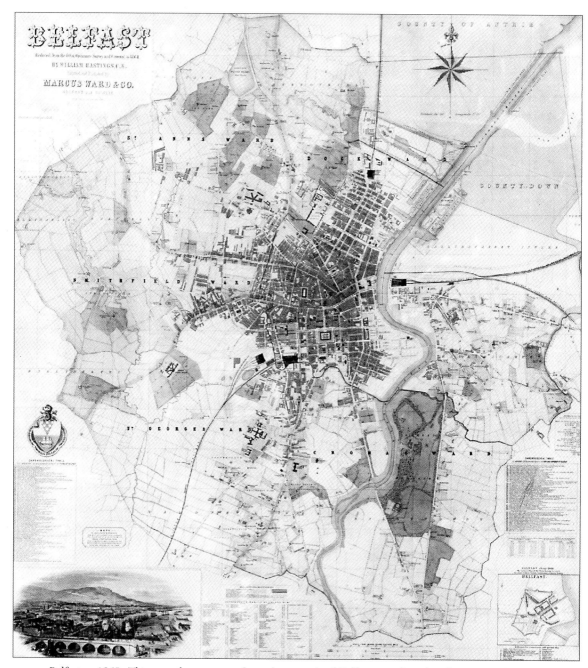

Belfast *c.* 1865. This map demonstrates how the growth of Belfast was shaped and constrained by the physical geography of the surrounding countryside. Hemmed in by the Antrim Plateau and the Castlereagh Hills and bounded to the east by the river Lagan, the city was forced to overflow along the Antrim and Down coasts of Belfast Lough. The cartouche in the lower left corner shows the new Queen's Bridge with Cave Hill in the distance, while the inset map opposite depicts the city in 1661.

INTRODUCTION

Nestling beneath the unmistakable contours of Cave Hill, the city of Belfast lies at the head of the broad valley that carries the River Lagan to Belfast Lough, between the Holywood and Castlereagh Hills to the south and the high moors of Divis and Black Mountain to the north, in a setting at once unique and eternally familiar. The city takes its name from a sandbank (in Irish *fertas*, later *Fersaid*) which forms a ford a little upstream from the mouth of the Lagan, where it is joined by the River Farset, also called after the ford. This was a place of great strategic importance, and was fortified by John de Courcey in the late twelfth century to protect the route between the two English strongholds at Downpatrick and Carrickfergus. The first records of human settlement date from the early fourteenth century and describe a castle, chapel and dwelling houses (called by the English 'the Ford') standing near to modern-day Castle Square. The first usages of the name 'Belfast' (from the Irish *Beal Feirste*, tr. 'approach to the sandbank') date from 1476, and are contained in several references to the taking and demolition of the castle called Belfast in fifteenth- and sixteenth-century chronicles.

During the sixteenth century the Tudor monarchy became increasingly determined to extend its rule in Ireland. To this end, Elizabeth I initiated a plan of settlement known as 'plantation', whereby tracts of land were granted to 'adventurers' to exploit and develop. In 1603 the 'castle of Bealfast' and its adjoining lands were granted to Sir Arthur Chichester, who later directed James I's plantation of Ulster in his role as King's Deputy in Ireland. Chichester rebuilt Belfast Castle, which he found in ruins on the banks of the Farset (now covered over, but still flowing underneath High Street; the curve of the road follows the course of the river) and started laying out his town, which in 1611 was described as being 'plotted out in good forme' with many families from England, Scotland and the Isle of Man already resident, and a good inn. In 1613 the town was granted a royal charter, making it a corporate borough and entitling it to send two members to the Irish parliament in Dublin, and Sir Arthur was made Baron Chichester of Belfast.

By the end of the seventeenth century Belfast had grown considerably in wealth and importance as a port and market town. Several of its merchants had made fortunes through trade with Europe and America, as well as Britain. One of them, 'Black

George' McCartney, gave the town its first water supply in the 1680s; at the same time, the ford across the Lagan was replaced by a bridge, the old Long Bridge of twenty-one arches, which was itself replaced by the Queen's Bridge in 1841.

During the reigns of the four Georges (1714–1830) Belfast changed out of all recognition. Its population, which stood at 8,000 in the mid-eighteenth century, doubled to almost 20,000 by 1800 and reached over 50,000 by 1830. Its trade increased greatly too and, although most of its prosperity still came from trade and commerce, the beginnings of industrial development had started to appear. Arthur Chichester, who inherited the title of Lord Donegall and Belfast with it in 1757, had initiated a series of improvements as he re-negotiated rents and leases. For example, he stipulated that all new buildings in the main streets were to have slate rather than thatched roofs, sash windows, walls of a certain height and width, and a paved area at the front. He also provided public buildings at his own expense, such as the Exchange in Corn Market and St Anne's Church in Donegall Street, and gave land for others, such as the Poor House (now Clifton House) and the White Linen Hall.

Although Belfast had started as an English settlement, it became more and more Scottish in character as it expanded, and most of its population, including the wealthy merchants, were Presbyterians who, like Catholics, were barred from membership of the Corporation that officially ran the town. These men set up their own institutions, such as the Charitable Society, which built and ran the Poor House, provided a much-needed graveyard at Friar's Bush, and an improved water supply. They built the White Linen Hall in 1783, formed one of the earliest Chambers of Commerce in Britain in the same year, and established the Linen Hall Library and Belfast Academy. In the 1780s and 1790s many became diverted by radical politics as Volunteers or United Irishmen, and not a few were punished for their part in the Rebellion of 1798. In the aftermath of the fighting and reprisals, however, the Presbyterian establishment came to accept the Act of Union (1800), which abolished the Dublin parliament and made Ireland part of the United Kingdom. The first banks in Belfast were established in the early 1800s, along with the Academical Institution and a number of still-extant societies, such as the Literary Society and the Natural History Society.

Between 1830 and 1880 Belfast changed from a thriving market town and commercial centre with some industry into a great industrial city. Although trade and commerce remained important and, indeed, grew as the town grew, they were increasingly replaced as the main source of wealth by manufacturing industry. Steam-powered mills and factories, steam-driven ships and railway trains, linen warehouses and shipyards were the signs of the new age. Long before the end of the century Belfast boasted the biggest port in Ireland in terms of the volume and value of trade, and the biggest linen factories, the largest ropeworks, and the greatest tonnage production of ships in the world.

Along with this industrialisation came urban growth. The physical size of Belfast increased enormously as the town boundary, fixed in the 1830s to enclose 2½ square miles, was extended to encompass 23 by the end of the century. This extension brought within the town boundary large numbers of people who had previously lived in suburbs such as Ballymacarrett; it also reflected an astonishing population explosion in which Belfast's population grew at a greater rate and in a shorter time than that of any comparable Victorian city. Starting at 53,000 in 1831, it reached 70,000 in 1841, 121,000 in 1861, and 208,000 in 1881, to stand at over 350,000 by the end of the century. As industry grew, and as the spread of the railway network made the journey easier and cheaper, thousands of people travelled from country areas to work and live in Belfast. As elsewhere, such rapid changes caused great social problems. In the case of Belfast, these were compounded by community divisions and the sectarian riots for which the town became notorious during this period.

Private charity and municipal provision worked hard to alleviate the appalling conditions endured by many of Belfast's inhabitants. Streets were paved and sewered, regulations introduced to govern markets, rubbish disposal, and standards of new housing, and Boards of Health appointed. Hospitals and schools were built for the poor.

Belfast was an unhealthy place, primarily because of its rapid industrial expansion and history as a port, which aided the introduction and spread of infectious diseases such as typhus and cholera, and also because of its low-lying situation, with hills on either side that captured and held the tons of airborne soot flowing from its coal-fired factory chimneys. During the nineteenth century well-to-do citizens escaped from the smog and germs in the city centre, where they had previously lived, by building fine houses in the fresher heights of areas such as Malone.

At the same time the Council embarked on an ambitious programme of city redevelopment. The wide thoroughfare of Victoria Street and Corporation Street was created in the 1850s, while Royal Avenue was completed in the 1880s to replace the jumble of narrow and decaying lanes which made up Hercules Street and its neighbours. Municipal gas lit these new streets, with the public purchase of the gas company (whose profits later paid for the City Hall). An ambitious plan of improvement was initiated by the newly constituted Harbour Commissioners, involving the cutting of a deep channel across the tidal sloblands of the Lagan approach to allow even the largest ships direct access to the city docks. The earth that this process threw up formed Queen's Island, which became part of Harland & Wolff's massively extended shipyards. Across the river gleamed the new Custom House and Harbour Office. Further into town, Belfast's citizens watched as buildings such as the Ulster Hall, the Presbyterian College, the Palm House, Crumlin Road Jail and the Courthouse made new marks on the city skyline. This remarkable boom continued after Belfast was officially accorded the status of City in 1888. Municipal services expanded with the introduction of electrification, a public transport system, a programme of public park provision and the reorganisation of emergency services such as the Fire Brigade and Ambulance Service. Pride in the city, its achievements and its ambitions was symbolised by the Council's acquisition of the site of the old White Linen Hall in 1890 to build a magnificent City Hall, which opened in 1906.

The photographs which follow document the changing face of Belfast since its emergence as a great Victorian city. Chosen from the collections of the Ulster Museum, which holds some of the most historically important photographic archives in Ireland, they reflect equally the development of the physical features and the social, cultural, economic and political landscape of the city during the century or so since 1855. The value of photographs as historic documents lies above all in the way that they allow the past to speak directly and with great familiarity. Although there are, of course, some things that they cannot reveal – the clatter of thousands of people going about their business, the smell and noise of industry, the rattle of transport and the sound of street cries and conversations – it is hoped that the images presented here will help our readers realise the rich variety of city life in Belfast over the last hundred years.

This image of the Harland & Wolff shipyard in 1911, with the *Titanic* under construction, a full order book and full employment, symbolises the extent of Belfast's pre-war industrial achievement.

SECTION ONE

SITE & CITY

Bird's-eye view of Belfast from Sydenham, c. 1863, showing the expansion of the harbour and docks and the concentrated growth of heavy industry on the southern side of the Lagan at Ballymacarrett.

Belfast from Cave Hill, 1878, looking south-east across the northern suburbs of the city to the hills of Co. Down. In the foreground, fields of cornstacks illustrate the still-rural character of the city at this time.

Belfast from Cave Hill, *c.* 1960, showing the pattern of housebuilding along the Antrim shore. The shipyards and associated industries are marked by the plume of smoke in the centre of the picture.

Belfast from Cave Hill, *c.* 1950, looking over the new housing estate of White City towards Co. Down, showing the creep of post-Second World War urban development along the north shore of Belfast Lough. Reputedly, the cave from which this picture was taken was used as a hiding place by fugitive United Irishmen after their abortive rising in 1798.

Royal Avenue from the top of the City Hall with Cave Hill and Napoleon's Nose in the distance. This photograph must have been taken before February 1954, when the electric trams which here dominate the city centre traffic were withdrawn from service.

Fall's Park, *c.* 1910, with the Black Mountain in the distance. The summit of this hill to the west of Belfast was later chosen as the site for the local television transmitter.

The Wolfhill Spinning Co., Mill Avenue, Ligoniel, 1936. A plentiful local water supply led to the establishment of at least two large linen mills on the hilly north-western outskirts of Belfast. This view shows how the rural character of their setting survived well into the twentieth century.

Harmony Village, Lignoniel, *c.* 1967, built to house millworkers. The well-found nature of this row of two-storey dwellings suggests that they were intended for elite employees, such as foremen or senior mechanics.

The Royal Damask Weaving Factory, Ardoyne village, *c.* 1910. Ardoyne also originally started out as a rural mill village. Note the roof lights of the shed on the left-hand side of this local factory, which produced fine linen on hand looms, instead of the power looms used in most urban centres.

Shaw's Bridge, 1905. Now a much-loved beauty spot, this fine stone bridge was built in the seventeenth century and provided the last opportunity for travellers to cross the Lagan between Belfast and Drumbridge in Co. Down, some 4 miles away.

The Lagan at Newforge, *c.* 1884. The Lagan connected Belfast with its rich hinterland to the south and west as well as providing power for industry. The towpath was a popular destination for a stroll in country-like surroundings.

The Lagan at Drumbridge, *c.* 1910. Barges were an important means of transporting bulky goods to and from Belfast. Here we see the barge *Shamrock* approaching Drumbridge, with Attie and Jane Mullen on board, and Johnny Douglas leading the horse.

Newforge Lane, *c.* 1900, viewed from Malone Road entrance and showing the thatched cottage that used to stand there.

A GROWING CITY

The Haypark Brickworks in Ava Avenue, September 1910, with Annadale Woods and the Stranmillis brickfields in the distance. Very little good building stone was readily available near Belfast so most dwelling houses were made of locally made brick. The extent of building needed to house Belfast's rapidly growing population is indicated by the amount of ground turned to this purpose.

Unveiling of the statue of the Earl of Belfast, November 1855, in College Square. This statue was the original 'Black Man', so-called because it was made of black metal. It was replaced in 1873 by the statue of Revd Dr Henry Cooke, the present 'Black Man'.

Donegall Square East, September 1874, showing Donegall Square Methodist Church, built in 1849, and, adjoining it on the right, a row of eighteenth-century Belfast merchants' residences.

Donegall Place looking towards Castle Place, 1872, shown before the removal in 1879 of the buildings at the end of the street to make way for the opening up of Royal Avenue.

Hercules Street, 1880, looking north at the north end of the street during its demolition in 1879 to make way for Royal Avenue. The buildings still standing on the left housed (from the corner up) a public house, a sawyer's, a plumber's, a chandler's, a soap and candle-maker's, and a sawmaker and repairer.

Frederick Street, *c.* 1896, showing what are generally regarded as the last thatched houses remaining in inner Belfast. Bunches and barrels of displayed carrots, cabbages and other vegetables proclaim the one on the left as a greengrocer's shop.

High Street at the junction with Skipper Street, *c.* 1888. According to the photographer, the house at the corner was known as the 'Bullock School', while the three houses to its left were originally one of the eighteenth-century town houses built by Belfast's owner, the Marquess of Donegall.

College Square East, 1930, showing the view from the roof of the Municipal College of Technology,
looking towards the Falls district of Belfast, marked by the twin spires of St Peter's Roman Catholic
Cathedral, seen in the centre distance.

A view of East Belfast, looking towards the Holywood Hills, from the top of the 150-ft high Ropeworks
chimney, 1921. The belfry tower of St Mark's Church, Dundela, is a conspicuous landmark. The
photographer had to be held by his coat-tails as the wind blew the camera to the ground. All survived!

Joy's Entry, 1929. During the commercial expansion of Belfast in the eighteenth century, the gardens of the merchants' houses on High Street, which ran to Anne Street, were given over to houses, workshops and stores. The paths between them became narrow passageways, called 'entries', frequented by street traders and hung with tradesmen's signs.

Chichester Street, c. 1905. Belfast also had its wide thoroughfares. This early view of a beautifully cobbled Chichester Street, with Montgomery Street to the left, takes the eye down to the hazy form of Fisherwick Church, seen at the bottom of the road in the distance.

Pottinger's Entry, 1901. Like Joy's Entry opposite, named for the first Henry Joy, founder of the *Belfast Newsletter*, the oldest still-published newspaper in the world, Pottinger's Entry also took its name from one of early Belfast's leading families. The Pottingers were prominent in the city after Thomas was made Sovereign in 1688, and are also commemorated by the Mount Pottinger district of east Belfast.

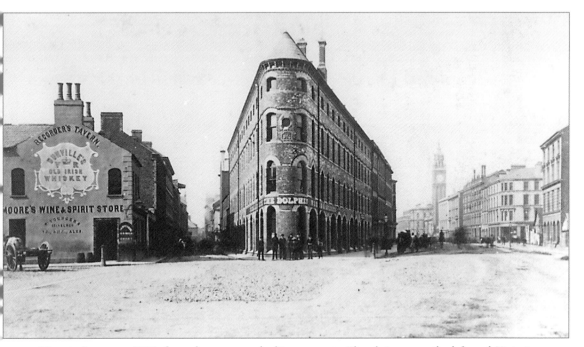

Victoria Square, *c.* 1880, from the entrance, looking across to Church Lane, on the left, and Victoria Street, with the famous triangular Dolphin Wine and Spirit House (now Bittles Bar) standing between the two. In the distance, the Albert Clock has already acquired a tilt, even at this early date.

Millfield, 1913. A street of old, two-storey dwelling houses and commercial premises, most long past their best. In 1908 the condition of working-class housing in Belfast was criticised so severely in a government report that the Corporation introduced a scheme for limited slum clearance under the Belfast Improvement Order of 1910.

Bloomfield Avenue, 1910, looking from the Newtownards Road. A more prosperous area than above, with solid bay-windowed terraced houses and neat shops.

Mitchell's Row, off Brown Square, 1912, one of the streets scheduled for revival under the 1910 Improvement Order, and listed in the street directories as 'four small houses', with no name or occupation ascribed to the occupants.

Pepper Hill Steps, leading to Pepper Hill Court on the south-east of Carrick Hill, seen during its demolition in 1894. Note the plaid shawls worn by the women at the top of the steps.

Lavinia Street, off the lower Ormeau Road, photographed in 1938 for the Concrete Piling Co. Ltd. These sturdy houses were built in the 1870s; the second door to the right led through to the back alley, a facility made compulsory in 1878 to allow direct access to privies.

Belfast Corporation housing at Twaddell Avenue, 1929. Belfast had the worst record of any British city for municipal housing between the wars when only 2,562 houses were built, none after 1930.

New Flats at Annadale on the Ormeau Embankment, *c.* 1964. Between 1948 and 1968 Belfast Corporation built 11,600 new dwellings in thirty development areas within the city as Belfast grew to bursting point within its boundaries.

Campbell's Place, off Staunton Street, May 1975. Even at this late date many Belfast working-class families continued to live in dark, damp, poorly found houses such as these.

HARBOUR & SHIPPING

Queen's Quay seen from the Lagan, c. 1900. By the end of the nineteenth century Belfast had become the largest port in Ireland, sending and receiving goods to and from all parts of the world. This picture shows a steam tug pulling barge-loads of coal to the gasworks upriver.

A general view of Belfast Docks with Cave Hill in the background, *c.* 1965, showing facilities for landing and off-loading freight.

Queen's Bridge with Queen's Quay behind, *c.* 1965. Behind the row of cranes at the Coal Quay can be seen the towering gantries of Harland & Wolff's shipyard. The public toilets which stood at the right of the Coffee Stand in the foreground have been removed by the photographer, leaving half a passer-by standing at the car beside the horse trough.

Laganbank Road, 1930, from an elevated position on Oxford Street, showing the barges that carried goods up the Lagan moored at the Sand Quay.

Queen's Bridge, *c.* 1910. The last of the line of horse-drawn carts in the foreground of this picture is taking one of the huge drying turbines produced in the Sirocco Works on the east side of the river to the docks for export.

Pollock Dock, 1935, seen from across the Lagan, showing the freight ship *Mount Prionas* unloading grain at the Pacific Flour Mills berth.

Donegall Quay, 1930, where passenger steamers on domestic routes to Scotland, England, the Isle of Man and the rest of Ireland traditionally docked. The wooden jetty in the foreground, built in 1887 and demolished in 1945, served the Bangor boats.

Clarendon Dock, 1938, showing sacks of potatoes being loaded on to the SS *Mardinian*. Seed and eating potatoes were important export commodities and the Ministry of Agriculture had a depot at the docks to check the quality of all sent out.

Clarendon Dock, 1917, with two sailing ships, one from Norway, and two steam tugs. The approach to Belfast Harbour was tidal and notoriously difficult, and all large ships wishing to enter and leave had to have their passage assisted and piloted.

Dutch dredger at work, 1921, clearing the low-water access channels which snaked between the mud banks and slobland at the entrance to Belfast Harbour.

Lighthouse One, technically termed the Holywood Bank Light 1, was built in 1844 by Alexander Mitchell, the blind Belfast engineer, to guide ships on Belfast Lough. Demolished in 1959, it had been the first building in Ireland whose foundations were secured by screw piles.

Chichester Street, 1915, showing the old toll house near the corner of Great Edward Street (now Victoria Street), originally used for collecting dues from boats entering May's Dock, which lay just above Canal Quay at the mouth of the Blackstaff River.

Belfast Harbour Office, Corporation Square, decorated for the coronation of King George V in 1911. The Harbour Office occupies the site of Connell's Dock, originally William Ritchie's shipyard, the first shipbuilding firm in Belfast.

Belfast Custom House, one of a number of Belfast buildings designed by the famous architect Charles Lanyon and completed in 1857, showing a line of carters and their horses standing in Custom House Square waiting for orders.

The Custom House Steps, *c.* 1900, known as Belfast's 'Speaker's Corner', where huge crowds gathered on Sundays to hear and watch budding politicians and preachers in action.

Cunard Line Offices, Albert Square, *c.* 1920, where agents James Little and Co. handled the Belfast trade for Cunard's trans-Atlantic service, whose great ships *Queen Mary* and *Queen Elizabeth* later became two of the most famous of British passenger liners.

Canadian Pacific's new offices at 24 Donegall Place, 1929, advertising freight and passenger rail and sea services, including winter 'Sunray' cruises to China and Japan.

The Bennett family before embarkation from Belfast Harbour, April 1929, one of a series of photographs of emigrant families commissioned by McCalla and Co., shipping agents.

The Foster family before emigration, April 1929. The difference in the prosperity of this family and the one portrayed above is clearly visible; emigration was part of the experience of Irish people of all classes and cultures.

BELFAST ON THE MOVE

The Queen's Quay terminal of the Belfast and Co. Down railway, shortly after the re-opening of the rebuilt station in 1912, showing the whole area decorated with greenery and crowds passing through barriers on to the platforms.

The Midland Railway station at York Street, 1933, advertising day trips to Portrush on Wednesdays, Saturdays and Sundays for 1s 6d third class and 2s 6d first class.

Queen's Quay station, 1894, showing the old building before the area barrier was removed and the front extended in the rebuilding of the station in 1912.

Great Northern Railway Terminus in Great Victoria Street, *c.* 1895. The signs 'Cars In' and 'Cars Out' on the imposing front entrance refer to horse-drawn jaunting or 'side' cars, such as the two parked at the lamp-post, rather than motor cars.

Great Victoria Street, 1976, showing the last remaining section of the original railway station with the Europa Hotel in the background.

Queen's Bridge, *c.* 1910, viewed from the entrance to Oxford Street and showing the steam locomotive *Alexandra* being transported by horse-drawn cart. This was being pulled by a team of six horses, but so well balanced were the one-horse lorries used by local haulage firms like the famous Wordie's that a single horse could pull loads of up to 3 tons.

Warning notice at Station Street, *c.* 1960, reminding carters to help their horses give their best effort when going uphill.

Wellington Place, 1902, showing horse-drawn trams and other traffic splashing through the Belfast floods of September that year, caused when the new sewer system failed to cope with a combination of unusually high tides and heavy rain.

Donegall Place, *c.* 1903, showing a Corporation 'scavenger' with shovel, brush and handcart sweeping up the tell-tale signs of horse-drawn trams.

Donegall Place, 1905. Laying lines for the new electric trams at the corner of Donegall Place and Castle Street.

'The New Illuminated Car' photographed for Belfast City Tramways in 1905, and produced as a postcard to commemorate the coming of the electric trams in that year.

Upper Newtownards Road, *c.* 1910, showing the old tram terminus at the city boundary, looking back towards Belfast from a point more or less opposite the present junction with Rosepark.

Queen's Road, 28 February 1954, showing the last tram to run on the Belfast Corporation tramways making its way to join the procession of tramcars to the Ardoyne Depot.

Queen's Road, *c.* 1920. A line of open-top electric trams, the first two travelling to the Antrim Road and Greencastle respectively, with an early charabanc-type car attracting curious glances from the walking crowds.

Donegall Square East, 1928, showing the car showrooms of the Belfast inventor and mechanical engineer Harry Ferguson, situated between the YMCA building and the classical façade of the Methodist Church.

MADE IN BELFAST

Donegall Place, showing the Trades Arch erected for the Royal Visit of 1885, with the White Linen Hall behind. Models of a loom, a steam engine and a ship testify to the main sectors of Belfast's industrial prosperity, while the motto on the pillar on the right asserts that 'Employment is Nature's Physician'.

Donegall Square North, *c.* 1890. Many of Belfast's more substantial buildings were originally erected to serve the linen trade, such as the workshop and linen warehouse of the Northern Spinning Co. Ltd, seen in the centre of this photograph.

Donegall Square, *c.* 1880. A panoramic view of Belfast's White Linen Hall, with its huge quadrangle where linen was traded from the eighteenth century. The large building partly obscured by trees on the right is the linen warehouse of Richardson Sons & Owdens, built at the height of the linen boom of the 1860s.

Crumlin Road Linen Mills and Weaving Factory, owned by William Ewart & Son Ltd, with a group of workers striking a jaunty pose at the door. Women and children, being cheaper to employ than men, predominated among workers in the linen industry.

York Street Flax Spinning Co., stretching into the distance at Henry Street. Founded in 1828 by Thomas Mulholland, the pioneer of linen production in the city, York Street Mill was, at the height of its business, the biggest linen mill in the world.

Weaving damask cloth on a Jaquard loom, *c.* 1920. The pattern on the cloth was carried by the punch cards hanging in swathes over the weaver, making the Jacquard loom one of the first pre-programmed machines in common use.

Spinning linen thread. Linen was spun wet, and conditions in the spinning mill, with its hot and humid atmosphere, were extremely unhealthy. Workers were constantly sprayed with water as the drenched flax fibres were twisted round the spindle, and generally went barefoot to avoid slipping on the soaked stone floor of the mill.

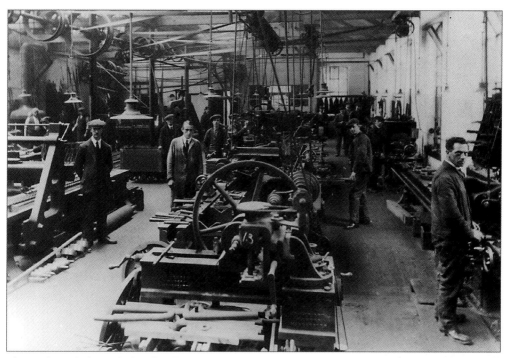

The Mechanics' Shop, Blackstaff Mill, *c.* 1920: an unusual photograph of men at work in a spinning mill.

Brookfield Linen Co. Ltd, Crumlin Road, *c.* 1911, showing a woman weaving plain linen for sheeting and suchlike. Weaving was an extremely hot and noisy process, made even more unhealthy because of the risk of injury from working so close to unguarded machinery.

Queen's Island, *c.* 1900, showing the launch of the *Statendam*, 10,000-ton sister ship to the *Rotterdam*, built by Harland and Wolff for the Holland-American Line.

The staircase and foyer on board a White Star liner, showing something of the opulence of the luxury ships built by Harland & Wolff.

Premises and workforce of Peter McKeown, Boatbuilder, Whitla Street, *c.* 1890, one of a number of smaller maritime concerns in the city.

The North Yard of the shipbuilding firm Workman & Clark, *c.* 1929. Popularly known as the 'Wee Yard', this company was located across the Lagan from Harland & Wolff, to the north of the Milewater basin, and went into liquidation in the 1930s.

Part of the great turning shop in Harland & Wolff's engine works, *c.* 1888. Note the electric overhead crane, shifting a big engine bed-plate, and the three big lathes on the right, dwarfing the workers standing beside them.

Queen's Road, 1911, showing shipyard workers leaving at the end of a shift, with the *Titanic* still in stocks in the background. At this time Harland & Wolff were at the height of pre-war production, employing over 14,000 men in their associated works.

The *Canberra*, built for the P&O line and launched in 1960, was the last of the great passenger liners built by Harland & Wolff.

The ill-fated White Star liner, the *Titanic*, seen here immediately after her launch on 31 May 1911 and before her distinctive four funnels had been fitted. She was perhaps the most famous of all the ships built in Belfast.

The Ropewalk, in the Belfast Ropework Co., Connswater, *c.* 1935. Founded in 1876, by the turn of the century this company was the largest of its kind in the world, with four factories covering nearly 40 acres in east Belfast, and a workforce of 3,000 men, women and children.

The end of another day, Belfast Ropeworks, 1905, showing workers leaving the factory by way of a footbridge over the River Connswater.

The interior of the Falls Foundry of Combe
Barbour in North Howard Street, 1928, showing
brass founding.

The foundry itself, *c*. 1911, with its fleet of lorries ready to move. Although the one third from the left
carries parts apparently destined for the Ford Motor Co., in Detroit, Michigan, the company was primarily
concerned with the manufacture of linen machinery such as spindles, hackling engines and so on.

Kiln of Ballymacarrett glassworks, 1930, in
the yard of Richardson's Chemical Manure
Co. Described at the time of its erection in
1785 as the largest in the British Isles, this
was the first and longest-lived of Belfast's
three such structures. It collapsed in October
1937.

The Linfield Road premises of Murray Sons & Co., tobacco and snuff manufacturers, seen from across the
railway sidings at Great Victoria Street station.

Gallaher's of York Street, showing the side entrance of the factory with the footpaths crowded with workers. Thomas Gallaher transferred his business from Derry to Belfast in 1863; by 1891 he had forty-five tobacco spinning machines at work in this building. He began making the cigarettes for which Gallahers was most well known in 1902.

Gallahers Ltd, York Street, 1932, showing women hand-stripping tobacco leaf in conditions that had changed little since the factory opened. The wooden stalls offered some protection against draughts.

The Shaftesbury Avenue London Office of the
Belfast whiskey distillers, Dunville & Co.,
c. 1905, whose custom-built premises on the
Grosvenor Road had lofts that could hold
6,000 tons of grain and fermenting vessels
that could hold 35,000 gallons of liquid each.
By this time Belfast was responsible for
almost 60 per cent of Irish whiskey exports.

Packing bottles at Lyle & Kinahan's, Cullingtree Road, *c.* 1920. One of the leading wine and spirit
merchants and beer bottlers in Belfast, Lyle & Kinahan's also manufactured aerated waters and had an
artesian well 250 ft below their premises.

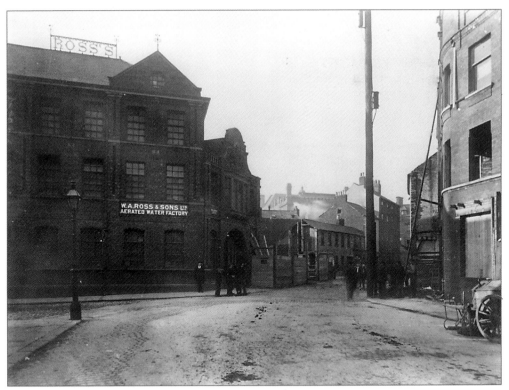

The William Street South home of W.A. Ross & Sons Ltd, still famous for its aerated and mineral waters.

The front exterior of another well-known Belfast lemonade maker, Grattan & Co., on Great Victoria Street, 1915.

Inglis & Co. Ltd's biscuit factory on the Newtownards Road, 1937. Now out of business, Inglis's was one of Belfast's best-known bakeries, producing a range of fancy cakes and biscuits as well as a variety of breads.

Bernard Hughes Model bakeries on Springfield Road, *c.* 1920. Unusually this company was successful at both flourmilling and baking. Like Inglis's, it has now ceased trading.

SHOPS & COMMERCE

Boys selling the Belfast Telegraph *near the Bank Buildings on Royal Avenue, c. 1920. The 'tele' boys with their distinctive cry still add colour to Belfast's main shopping streets, although they tend nowadays to be a bit older than the two lads pictured here.*

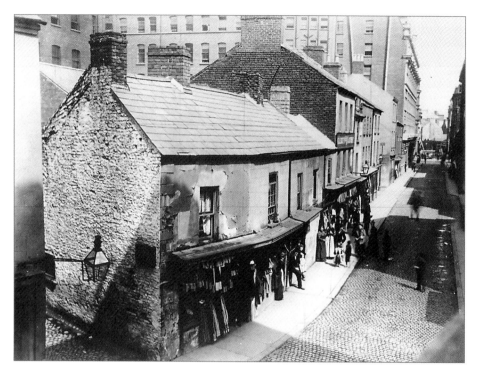

Berry Street, 1894, showing a row of shops selling second-hand clothes. This trade was enormously important in Belfast, where so many women worked long hours in mill and factory, and large quantities of apparel were imported from Glasgow to meet local demand.

High Street, 1894, looking down Skipper Street, showing a range of commercial premises dealing in (from left to right) stationery, bookbinding, saddlery, watchmaking and jewellery.

Smithfield Market, 1950s. Two
little boys reach out to each other
opposite Harry Hall's bookshop,
one of the best-remembered sites
in the old Smithfield.

Smithfield Market, May 1974.
Passers-by stare at the smouldering
remains of shops on the south-east
corner of Smithfield Market,
shortly after its destruction by fire
on 7 May.

Donegall Place from the grounds of the White Linen Hall, 1890, showing the corner of Robinson & Cleaver's, one of Belfast's largest and most opulent stores, famous for the supply of top-quality Irish linen to discerning customers around the globe.

The imposing marble staircase leading from the ground floor of Robinson & Cleaver's, now in a private mansion.

The Castle Place and Lombard Street façades of J. Robb & Co. Ltd, Hosier, Furrier and Costumier, *c.* 1910.

Inside Robb's shop, showing the hosiery department, *c.* 1930. Notice the lattice of pipes at ceiling height, used to convey the cashboxes carrying money and bills of purchase from the various departments to the cashier's office, and the change and receipts back to the customers.

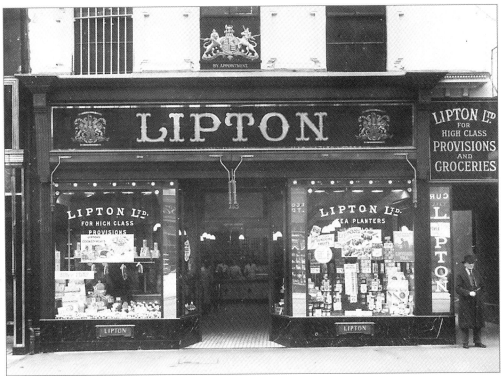

Lipton Ltd, High Class Provisions and Groceries, in High Street, 1936, one of a chain of stores founded originally on the tea trade enterprises of Thomas Lipton, who became a close friend of Edward VII and whose yacht *Shamrock* was a familiar sight in Belfast Lough.

Stewart's Cash Stores on the Antrim Road, 1938, showing the covered fruit stall at the front of the shop. This was the first of what eventually became one of Northern Ireland's biggest supermarket chains.

F.W. Woolworth and Co. Ltd, High Street, photographed in October 1929 when the building was under construction. Note the signs promising that the shop will be open for Christmas, and the banner advertising an amateur boxing contest between Ireland and Scotland at the Ulster Hall on Halloween night.

The finished building, June 1930.

Interior of Belfast Co-operative Society Shop no. 283 on the Ormeau Road, 1935, with its impressive display of Heinz baked beans. Notice the sign inviting customers to 'Serve Yourself' at a cost of 2d, 3d or 5d per tin, and the other Heinz products, such as salad cream, being advertised in the background.

The huge main premises of the Belfast Co-op on York Street, built in sections just before the First World War and shown here in 1919.

One of several small Co-op grocers in Belfast, this one was situated at 97 Woodvale Road, and the shopkeeper and his staff are seen here posing at the doorway. Among the items included in the window displays are carbolic soap, margarine, and 'Nerva' tonic. The Co-op also had its own bakery and dairy, through which outlets were supplied with milk, butter, and a variety of breads, cakes and biscuits.

The exhibition stand of Gilmore & Co., electrical suppliers, at the Royal Ulster Agricultural Society showgrounds in Balmoral, 1934, displaying a range of the most modern washing machines and refrigerators. Electricity had been available in Belfast since 1898, from a generating station in East Bridge Street. The opening of the Harbour Power Station in 1923 enabled domestic consumers not only in Belfast but also in Lisburn, Bangor and Holywood to be connected to the grid.

The A&F Corner, Radio and Electrical Engineers, on Shaftesbury Square, photographed in 1938. Note the hoarding on the wall above the shop advertising Phillips 'Motoradio', for 'music while you drive'.

St George's Market, 1975, showing the East Bridge Street façade, 1975. This is the last of Belfast's many market buildings to survive in its original state.

St George's Market, 1899, showing the remnant and old clothes section with a number of respectably dressed and hatted ladies inspecting minutely the quality of the material on offer.

The Pork Market, Oxford Street, *c.* 1910. Belfast was an important centre for the distribution of all kinds of agricultural produce and livestock. Here a cartload of dead pigs waits to be unloaded. Notice the horse's leather nosebag hanging at the front of the cart.

Flower seller, City Hall, *c.* 1950: an enduring image of the character of downtown commercial Belfast at almost any time until the 1960s.

HOTELS & CAFÉS

Milk Bar, Lombard Street, 1938. The Milk Bar was part of the Lombard Café, 'a first-class temperance restaurant', open from early morning to early evening. The inclusion of croissants on a pre-war Belfast menu raises a question, and perhaps an eyebrow.

The Dub Tearooms, Upper Malone Road, *c.* 1910, served townsfolk who took walks in Malone Gardens, many having travelled out of the city by tram to the nearby terminus.

The Carlton Café, Donegall Place, 1931. At the end of the nineteenth century these premises housed the Belfast Fur House, which sold 'invaluable garments for preserving the health in our rigorous climate'. The stained glass canopy along the front signalled its conversion to the Carlton Café in the early 1920s.

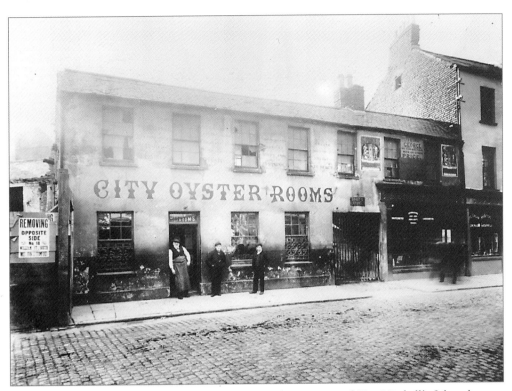

City Oyster Rooms, William Street South, *c.* 1902. This was one of Mrs Mitchell's fish and oyster establishments in the city which had clearly seen busier days . . . perhaps there was no 'R' in the month?

Venetian Café, Church Lane, 1935. The Venetian, owned in the early 1920s by C. Fusco, was one of several cafés owned by Italian immigrants throughout the north of Ireland, some of whom were interned when war broke out in 1939. The café itself became a casualty of war, being demolished in the devastating air raids on Belfast in April and May 1941.

McManus's Hotel and Stabling Yard, and the Pound, Townhall Street, 1912. One of the many establishments founded to cater for patrons of Belfast's livestock markets, the Pound Bar survived as a lively music pub opposite Oxford Street bus station until well into the 1970s.

The Royal Hotel, Donegall Square North, 1881. Built in 1785, this was the town house of the 2nd Marquess of Donegall before it became a hotel in about 1820, under the management of a former butler to the Donegall family. Guests included Charles Dickens, Daniel O'Connell and William Thackeray, who thought it 'as comfortable and well-ordered an establishment as the most fashionable cockney can desire'.

Grand Central Hotel, Royal Avenue, 1929. Built during the development of Royal Avenue in the early 1890s, this prestigious 200-room hotel remained a prominent city landmark until it was demolished in 1985. It was used during its last ten years as British army city-centre headquarters.

Talbot Bar and City Toilet Club, Arthur Square, 1906, shortly before their demolition for the erection of Mayfair Buildings.

Hugh Gray's Bar, Pilot Street, *c.* 1930. The be-suited men and cars lined up outside a dockside bar create a scene slightly reminiscent of Bonnie and Clyde.

Ulster Tavern, Chichester Street, *c.* 1930. The half-timbered mock-Tudor-style exterior of this building presents an incongruous backdrop for a policeman posted on points duty, especially when the only traffic appears to be a horse carriage going in the opposite direction.

The Gin Palace, Royal Avenue, *c.* 1908: another of Belfast's landmark bars, situated at the corner of Royal Avenue and North Street.

The XL Cafe and Restaurant, Arthur Square, 1938. This was one of two vegetarian XL cafés in the city. It was located on the first floor of a semi-circular building, the ground floor of which was originally the Grand Hotel and Café but later became Mooney's Bar, shown here, which closed in 1980.

THEATRES &
PICTURE HOUSES

Alhambra Picture House, North Street, December 1937. It had been opened in 1872 as the Alhambra Theatre by Dan Lowry, who had already opened similar variety halls in Liverpool and Manchester. At the time the photograph was taken, it had just become a cinema, reputedly the only one in Belfast where you could drink at the bar and watch the film. It was appropiate that The Charge of the Light Brigade, *starring Errol Flynn, was one of its first films. Flynn's father was Professor of Zoology at The Queen's University, Belfast 1931–48.*

Kelvin Picture Palace, College Square East, *c.* 1911. This is the earliest-known photograph of a Belfast cinema and shows the Kelvin the year after it opened. Named after William Thomson, Lord Kelvin, the famous scientist and inventor who was born in this terrace of houses in 1824 and spent his early years there, by the 1960s it had become the News and Cartoon Theatre.

Empire Theatre, Victoria Square, 1912. Home to the first films shown in Belfast in 1896, and the first theatre broadcast in Ireland in 1937, as the Empire Theatre of Varieties it had attracted leading music hall stars such as Marie Lloyd, George Formby, and Little Tich.

Theatre Royal, Arthur Street. The first
Theatre Royal, which opened on this site in
1793, was renowned as much for its dinginess
('the odour of mingled oranges and escaped
gas') as for its performances, though the
celebrated Mrs Siddons is known to have
played there on three occasions. This arcaded
four-storey building opened in 1871 but
burned down in June 1881. It was quickly
refurbished and by 1915 had become the
Royal Cinema.

The Grand Opera House, 1905, opened in 1895 carrying the legend 'cirque and Grand Opera House',
and circuses were indeed staged there between 1904 and 1909. Internally the theatre is a series of
marvellous curiosities, including the famous boxes supported by golden elephants. Located across the
road from the Europa ('the most bombed hotel in Europe') it suffered damage from several terrorist
attacks, being carefully restored each time.

Plaza Ballroom, Chichester Street, 1935. This distinctive building, with its end pavilions and central oriel surmounted by a shamrock-shaped pediment, was rebuilt in 1906 as the Royal Victoria Horse and Carriage Bazaar. By 1930 it was Belfast Plaza's Palais de Danse, and remained one of Belfast's main centres of nightlife until recent times.

The Royal Hippodrome, Great Victoria Street. Originally a terrace of four five-storey late Georgian houses, the scaffolding at the main doors betokens the completion of this new theatre in 1906–7. As well as being a theatre, it also screened films from early in the silent era before becoming a full-time cinema in 1931. It was renamed the Odeon in 1961, the New Vic in 1974 and demolished in the mid-1990s.

The Ritz, Fisherwick Place, 1936. Photographed here when it opened, the Ritz was the largest cinema in Northern Ireland, seating over 2,200 and claiming to have the biggest projection box in Europe. In 1963 it became the ABC. It was demolished in 1993, shortly after its closure.

Picturedrome Cinema, Mountpottinger Road, 1935: one of several luxury cinemas which opened in Belfast in the 1930s following the dramatically quick introduction of talkies from 1929.

The Broadway, Falls Road, April 1937, with uniformed attendants standing near the main entrance.

Stadium Cinema, Shankill Road, November 1937, showing the impressive foyer of a popular cinema immortalised in Van Morrison's 'Brown-eyed Girl'.

PUBLIC & MUNICIPAL PROVISION, EMERGENCY SERVICES & THE LAW

The almost-finished Belfast City Hall surrounded by advertising hoardings. Built as a monument to civic pride between 1898 and 1906, Belfast's magnificent City Hall was designed by the architect Alfred Brumwell Thomas and built by the local firm H. & J. Martin. Its imposing exterior of Portland stone, matched by fine marble interiors, celebrated the city's remarkable recent growth – by 1900 it had become the fastest-growing city in the British Isles.

City Hall under construction, 1903. The City Hall was constructed on the site of the White Linen Hall, built in 1783 to serve the linen trade, which along with shipbuilding formed the basis for Belfast's development and its eventual recognition as a city in 1888.

Albert Clock under construction, 1865–9. Officially named the Albert Memorial, the Albert Clock was designed by the local architect W. J. Barre and remains one of the city's best-known landmarks. Completed in 1869 as a memorial to the late Prince Consort, it was subsequently noticed to be 'considerably out of plumb'. By 1900 it had the distinct Tower of Pisa-like tilt which is still its hallmark. More than one local wag has been tempted to observe that this 113 ft-high clock tower has both the time and the inclination. . . .

Ulster Hall, Bedford Street. When first opened in 1862, this was one of the largest music halls in the British Isles, capable of holding 250 performers and an audience of over 2,000. The famous Victorian Mulholland organ dominates the stage. The cast-iron veranda, seen here, was removed in 1992, following severe bomb damage. Until the opening of the Waterfront Hall in January 1997, this remained the city's main concert hall.

BBC House, 31 Linenhall Street. The BBC began broadcasting from this building on 15 September 1924. The first voice to be heard was that of Tyrone Guthrie, then embarking on what would become a glittering career as actor and director.

Ulster Museum, Stranmillis Road. Opened in 1929 on ground acquired in the Botanic Gardens in 1912, the Belfast Municipal Museum and Art Gallery inherited the collections of the first Belfast Museum, established in 1831. In 1961 it was renamed the Ulster Museum by Act of Parliament, and became Northern Ireland's first National Museum.

King's Hall, Balmoral, 1934. Built in the early 1930s as the venue for the annual Royal Ulster Agricultural Society show held in May each year, one of the main events of Ulster's agricultural industry, in recent years it has also served as a trade exhibition and concert hall.

Palm House, Botanic Gardens. The Botanic Gardens were opened in 1820 with the aim of 'promoting a taste for horticulture'. They were taken over by the Belfast Corporation in 1894 as part of its policy of providing public parks. The Palm House, with its continuous colourful display throughout the year, remains a constant attraction.

Dunville Park, Falls Road. This 4-acre park was given to the city in 1869 by the Dunville family, Belfast distillers. The Doulton Fountain, in the foreground, was presented in 1891 by another Dunville, Robert Grimshaw, in memory of his sister, Sara.

Floral Hall, Bellevue, 1936. The Floral Hall at Bellevue, in north Belfast, near Belfast Zoo, was one of the city's most popular venues for dances.

Victoria Park, c. 1960. Built and given to the city as a 'People's Park', Victoria Park was completed in 1856 and sits on 50 acres of a 300-acre site on the foreshore of the Co. Down side of the Lagan that was bought for reclamation by Belfast Harbour Commissioners in 1854.

Corporation Baths, Falls Road, 1905. This new public leisure facility was opened in 1896. One of the first superintendents was a remarkable man called Alexander Bowman, who dedicated his life to service to others. The bare-footed boy on the pavement would, with all the other bathers, have had to wash his feet before his swim, one of the measures Bowman introduced.

Grove Park, York Road: an early photograph of what would later become the Grove Playing Fields, still a popular venue for park football, summer and winter, and home to the Grove Baths, Belfast's first international-size public indoor swimming pool.

Electricity Station, East Bridge Street. Belfast received its first electricity supply from a small, makeshift station in Chapel Lane in 1895, which provided power only for street lights. Within three years demand had so far outstripped supply that a new purpose-built power station, pictured here in 1938, was built to supply all the city's needs.

Harbour Power Station, 1936. Recommended in 1911, agreed and begun in 1918 with a grant of £150,000 from the Treasury, the first section of Belfast's second power station was opened by the Duke of Abercorn in 1923. It continued to supply power to Belfast and surrounding towns until Ballylumford Power Station went on line in the 1950s.

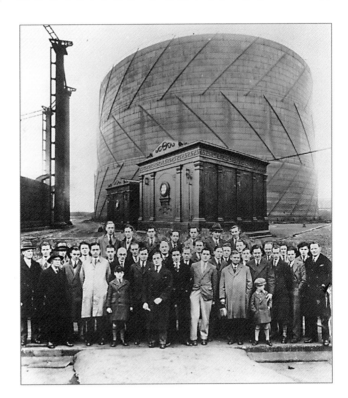

Gas Works, Ormeau Road. Members of the Belfast Textile Association on what appears to be . . . whoopee, a day out at Belfast Gasworks! The buildings date from the period 1887–91. The original gas works, one of the first in Britain, were built in 1823 and were bought by Belfast Council in 1874 for the princely sum of £423,000.

Belfast Corporation Gas Showrooms, Queen Street, 1939, showing a range of up-to-the-minute cookers. By 1928 Belfast Corporation Gas Department was producing 16.5 million cubic ft of gas a day, more than the first private company had produced in a year. Though the price paid by Belfast consumers was among the lowest in the United Kingdom, the Gas Department's profits were great enough to subsidise the rates, electricity, libraries, parks and public baths.

Telephone House, Cromac Street, 1935.
Opened in 1934 and shown here floodlit and
topped with a massive crown of lights to
celebrate King George V's Jubilee, this six-
storey building served as Belfast's telephone
exchange.

Belfast Post Office, Royal Avenue, *c.* 1960. Built in 1886 of Dungannon stone, the General Post Office
was acknowledged from the outset as being 'anything but ornate'.

Law Courts, Chichester Street. The Royal Courts of Justice had just been completed when this photograph was taken in 1933. The steel-framed Portland stone and Corinthian columns mask the equally stately marble legal halls which echo in the best Old Bailey traditions.

Castle Place, judge's equipage, 1917. The last judge to use the flamboyant equipage, supplied by Thomas Johnston & Sons, Belfast, and seen here outside the Ulster Club building, was Judge Moore of Moore Lodge, Kilrea, Co. Londonderry.

Fire Brigade headquarters, Chichester Street, Belfast, *c.* 1925. Following the reorganisation of the city's Fire Brigade, a new Brigade headquarters, with a model layout of engine room, offices, gymnasium, dormitories, watch room and workshops, was erected and opened in May 1894, together with twenty-seven houses for firemen and their families.

Horse-drawn steam pump, *c.* 1900, being driven along Chichester Street by Fire Brigade officers. The horses, which were shod only with light toe pieces to give their feet more grip on the square setts of Belfast's streets, were replaced with motors in 1910, which cut the time taken to reach fires by an average of 50 per cent.

Fire Brigade ambulance, *c.* 1900. Belfast's system, which combined fire and ambulance services, was the first of its kind in the British Isles and was followed by most other major cities until the 1940s.

Lifeboat Day, 1930. A lifeboat being drawn down High Street on one of the early Lifeboat Days, introduced to raise funds for the Royal National Lifeboat Institution, which is still entirely dependent on voluntary contributions.

RUC Barracks, Musgrave Street, 1939. The busiest and most central of Belfast's barracks, the huge garage at RUC Musgrave Street was home to a well-maintained range of police vehicles. Note the broad span of the Belfast roof, designed to cover the maximum space with the least support.

'Pickpockets harvest', Celtic Park, Falls Road, February 1912. Three Royal Irish Constabulary policemen are holding some of over 100 empty purses and wallets found the morning after a huge Home Rule meeting had been addressed in Celtic Park by Winston Churchill, then Home Secretary in the Liberal administration.

EDUCATION

Signwriting class in Belfast College of Technology, 1910. Although provision for its citizens varied considerably, Belfast has a long and proud belief in the importance of learning and literacy. That the 'nation' referred to in the motto here was Ireland as a whole is indicated by the welcome in Irish below, and by the Celtic design on the right.

Methodist College, Malone Road, *c.* 1900, established in 1868 as a public school for boarders and day pupils regardless of sex or religious persuasion, photographed here with its extensive grounds still intact at the right of the picture.

Royal Belfast Academical Institution, College Square East, 1902, was founded in 1810 as a university-level college as well as a school. This full view of the school buildings was taken before work started on the new Municipal College of Technology on ground leased in perpetuity by the Institute's governors in 1900, and which now completely obscures the right-hand side of this impressive building.

Nelson Street National School, 1902. A national system of primary education, intended to educate poorer children to basic standards of literacy and numeracy, was introduced in Ireland in 1831. By 1900 there were 8,684 National Schools in the country, many of them old and in extremely poor condition. This photograph, like the one below, was one of a series published in the *Belfast Weekly Telegraph* to support Dr W.A. McKeown's campaign highlighting the disgraceful surroundings in which the city's working-class children were being taught.

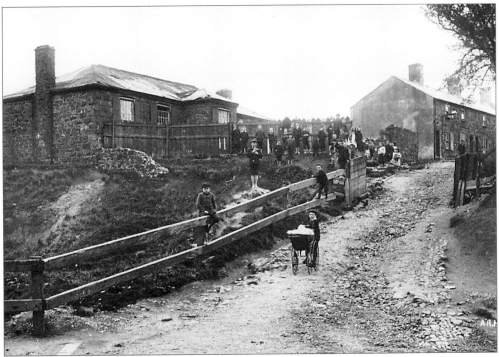

Springfield National School, Springfield Village, 1902. This school had 178 pupils on its roll though its only room could hold no more than 125. The original newspaper caption remarked on '. . . the squalor and wretchedness, the broken walls, the patched windows, the children with bare legs and feet huddled together. . . .'

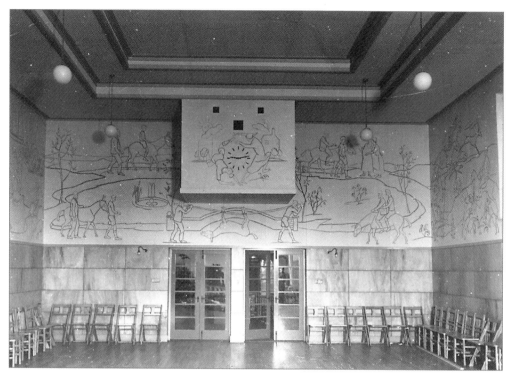

Edenderry Public Elementary School, Tennent Street, 1938, showing murals over the entrance to the Assembly Hall. It was one of the modern, large schools established by the Belfast Education Committee to replace the fifty city schools it had been forced to close down after 1923, as they were 'a direct menace to the health and physical development of the children'.

North Road Public Elementary School (later Strandtown Primary School), 1931. Another of the Corporation's new schools, built in the 1920s to the latest design and standing in extensive landscaped grounds.

Queen's University, *c.* 1920, showing the front façade of the main building as seen from Queen's Elms. Designed in 1845 by Charles Lanyon, who modelled it on the colleges of Oxford, and completed in 1849, Queen's University was one of the three Irish 'Queen's Colleges' established by Act of Parliament in 1845.

Stranmillis College, 1930, was built as a state training college for male and female primary teachers in 1922. It originally provided training for both Protestant and Catholic teachers, but pressure from the Catholic Church in particular led to the establishment of separate institutions for each faith, and the continuation of Stranmillis as a Protestant institution.

Municipal Technical College, *c.* 1960. The activities of the first Belfast Technical Colleges, where day and evening classes were given in a range of practical and vocational subjects, were originally scattered in a number of very unsatisfactory premises, including converted distilleries, hospitals and warehouses. This splendid purpose-built building was commissioned by Belfast Corporation in 1901 and welcomed its first pupils in 1907.

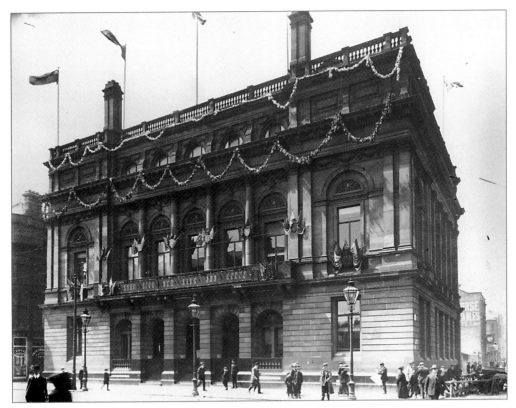

Free Public Library, Royal Avenue, shown here decorated either for the Royal Visit of 1903 or the Proclamation of the new King George V in 1910. Now known as Belfast Central Library, this grand library was built for the citizens of Belfast in 1869 as part of the mid-nineteenth-century municipal expansion of the city.

The Linenhall Library, Donegall Square North, 1937: the new premises of the original Belfast Library, founded in 1788 by the Belfast Society for Promoting Knowledge. The first librarian was the United Irishman, Thomas Russell, who was hanged for his part in Robert Emmet's rebellion of 1803 and later immortalised in verse by Florence Wilson as 'The-Man-from-God-Knows-Where'.

Belfast Mercantile College, Glenravel Street, *c.* 1920. Established in 1854, the college offered teaching at Commercial, Intermediate and Preparatory level. By 1937 it also had a separate Business Training School in an adjacent building.

The Underwood School of Shorthand and Typewriting, Wellington Place, *c.* 1920. Indicative of the growing importance of Belfast's clerical and secretarial sector in the years after the First World War, the ground floor of this establishment was given over to the sale of Underwood's Typewriters as 'the machine you will eventually buy'.

RELIGION, HEALTH & WELFARE

'Getting our picture took', c. 1903. Despite its condescending title and obvious staginess, this powerful image, which was taken to publicise the work of Belfast Central Mission, gives a real idea of what it was like to be a poor child in Belfast in the early 1900s. The can carried by the middle boy was for tea, which the Mission provided free or for a minimal charge.

The Poorhouse, North Queen Street, *c.* 1880. Belfast's oldest and, some would say, finest public building, the Poorhouse was built in the early 1770s by the Belfast Charitable Institute from a design submitted by the then editor of the *Belfast Newsletter* and millowner Robert Joy. Now known as Clifton House, it continues to be used for its original purpose, as a charitable home for old people.

Carrick House, Lower Regent Street, *c.* 1905. Built to accommodate the growing need for cheap and decent lodgings for working men, Carrick House was built by Belfast Corporation and opened in 1902. Tickets for beds, each costing 6*d*, were bought on a daily basis.

Brickworks, Springfield Road, *c.* 1908: homeless men sleeping rough in the heat that remained in the kilns after bricks were fired. This photograph was taken at 3.30 a.m. and was another of the images commissioned by Belfast Central Mission.

Presbyterian War Memorial Hostel, Howard Street: an interior view of one of the surprisingly well-appointed bedrooms available in the Presbyterian War Memorial Hostel. It was built in the early 1920s on the site of the ominously named House of Correction, with its grim notice 'Within amend, without beware'.

City Morgue, Victoria Square, *c.* 1886, with the premises of Cantrell & Cochrane behind, located in what was previously the Town Hall. The morgue was used to hold the anonymous or unclaimed bodies of those who had died in the street or were found alone as corpses.

Union Children's Infirmary, Lisburn Road, 1909. The opening ceremony of the new children's hospital at the Belfast Union Workhouse. Opened in May 1841 under the new Poor Law Act, the Workhouse included a Fever Hospital capable of holding 450 patients, schools to accommodate 400 children, several infirmaries and a lunatic ward.

Royal Victoria Hospital, Grosvenor Road, 1903. The Royal Victoria Hospital, originally the Belfast General Hospital, established in 1797, moved from Frederick Street to its new premises on the Grosvenor Road in 1903. It is seen here decorated for the official opening in July by King Edward VII and Queen Alexandra.

The Mater Infirmorum Hospital, Crumlin Road. Founded in 1883 and run by the Sisters of Mercy, it was supported by voluntary contributions and open for patients of all denominations. It contained, as well as 165 beds, a Hospice for the Dying and a Nurses' Home, all built for £50,000.

Elim Pentecostal Tabernacle, Hunter Street, April 1932 showing the evangelical preacher W. I. Kemp, addressing a crowd of worshippers and onlookers at the re-opening of premises, formerly a laundry, inaugurated by the Elim Pentecostal Alliance *c.* 1916.

Interior, Elim Pentecostal Tabernacle, Hunter Street, 1935. The austerity of surroundings, carried to an extreme here, is a common feature of gospel halls, where nothing should detract listeners from the Word.

St Anne's Cathedral, 1932. The artist Gertrude Martin at work in creating a mosaic of St Patrick in St Anne's Cathedral to mark the 1,500th anniversary of the traditionally accepted date of the saint's arrival in Ireland. The two images at either side of St Patrick represent pagan and Christian Ireland.

An interior view of the Holy Redeemer Roman Catholic Church, Clonard Gardens, in 1910, showing its beautiful altar during the celebration of Mass.

Carlisle Circus and Clifton Street, 1905, showing the impressive gothic piles of St Enoch's Presbyterian Church, completed in 1872, and Carlisle Memorial Methodist Church, completed in 1875, in the welter of nonconformist church building which followed the disestablishment of the Church of Ireland in 1869. The rubble in the foreground was caused by work on the electrification of the Belfast tramways.

POLITICS, WAR & PARADES

One of several ceremonial arches erected in Belfast on the occasion of the visit to the city in 1885 by the Prince and Princess of Wales, later Edward VII and Queen Alexandra, under which their procession through the streets would pass.

Orange Arch, Nelson Street, July 1912. Anti-Home Rule feeling among the Protestant population was at its height when this old-style Orange arch, with its garlands of flowers, was erected by the residents of this dockland street. The policeman is one of the few members of the crowd wearing shoes.

Orange March, Shaftesbury Square, 1923: a panoramic view of the parade stretching down the Dublin Road, with banners marking each participating Orange Lodge.

Unionist Convention, Caledonia Street (now Rugby Road), June 1892, when 12,000 delegates elected by Unionist associations across the province met in specially constructed halls near Stranmillis to voice their opposition to the second Home Rule Bill. Note the patriotic sign in Irish, 'Erin Go Bragh'.

Covenant Day, Donegall Place, 29 September 1912: crowds queueing to enter the City Hall to sign the Solemn League and Covenant on Ulster Day, in a concentrated declaration of opposition to Home Rule. Signatories were admitted in batches of 500, with 150 signing every minute.

Donegall Place, May 1915, showing the 36th (Ulster) Division parading past the City Hall, May 1915, prior to their departure for France. The ambulances that held stage when this photograph was taken remind us that over 5,500 men from this Division would be killed on the first two days of the Battle of the Somme, 1–2 July 1916.

Royal Avenue, 1901. Crowds gathered in front of the Provincial Bank of Ireland, Royal Avenue (the best venue before the City Hall was constructed five years later) to welcome home Boer War volunteers.

UVF Rally, Shaw's Bridge, 1913. The passing of the third Home Rule Bill saw Protestant opposition channelled increasingly into the Ulster Volunteer Force, which was sworn to armed resistance. In the event, the outbreak of the First World War in 1914 put off the day of reckoning for which the UVF had prepared in rallies such as this throughout Ulster.

High Street on Peace Day, 1919. The horror of the war just past and the ongoing bitterness of the conflict in Ireland cast a cold shadow over celebrations to mark the end of hostilities with Germany. Nevertheless Belfast made a brave and colourful effort, with its decorated streets, buildings and even trams.

Stormont Estate, 1936, showing the newly built Parliament Buildings on the far left, the Speaker's House in the centre and Stormont Castle, the official residence of the Prime Minister, on the right. The estate, originally called 'Storm Mount' (hence the name), was purchased from the Cleland family by the British government and presented to Northern Ireland after the passing in 1920 of the Government of Ireland Act, which established the Northern Ireland administration.

Royal Opening of Parliament. The newly created parliament for Northern Ireland being addressed in Belfast City Hall by King George V on 22 June 1921. It met there only once, moving to the Assembly's College of the Presbyterian Church in Ireland. The ceremony was boycotted by all shades of Nationalist representation. Security was intense, amid fears for the safety of the royal couple. 'I can't tell you how glad I am I came' said the king, 'but you know my entourage were very much against it'.

Carson's funeral, 1935. Edward, Baron Carson of Duncairn, was given a state funeral on 26 October 1935 and buried in St Anne's Cathedral. Here the gun carriage bearing the coffin enters Victoria Street from Queen's Square, drawn by ratings of the Ulster Division, Royal Naval Volunteer Reserve.

Stormont Estate, 1936. This famous statue of Lord Carson beckoning to his people stands at the top of the mile-long drive from the gates of the Stormont estate, with Parliament Buildings as a backdrop. In fact, Carson had initially opposed Home Rule for any part of Ireland and would have been all too aware of the irony of his statue appearing to proclaim the devolved Stormont administration. Just as curiously, Carson is the only British politician believed to have been present at the unveiling of his own monument – in 1933, two years before his death.

Stranmillis Allotments, 1917. Stranmillis was one of the greenfield areas in Belfast turned over to 'dig for victory' during the First World War. The Belfast Garden Plots Association carried on the work after the war.

Wartime Flax Culture, Fortwilliam Golf Course, 1917, showing de-seeded flax drying in sheaves on one of the greens that had been devoted to its cultivation by a patriotic membership. The 'fighting fibre' was much in demand for use in ships and, crucially, in the outfitting of aeroplanes towards the end of the war.

High Street burning during the Belfast Blitz, May 1941. Because it was felt that Belfast was too remote to be threatened by the Luftwaffe, the city was woefully unprepared for air attack. The fall of France brought it within range, and the city suffered its first raids in April 1941. The bombers returned the following month, when they targeted industrial and commercial areas in the city, causing extensive damage, particularly to the shipyard.

Westbourne Street after the Blitz, June 1941. Two months after the bombs fell a bed still sits forlornly in the midst of a devastated street. It has remained a puzzle why so many residential areas were hit during Belfast's first air raid, leaving behind over 900 fatalities, more in one night than in any British city outside London. The May raid killed 'only' 199.

ACKNOWLEDGEMENTS

The authors would like to thank the following people for their invaluable help and support in producing this book. While all of our colleagues in the Division of Human History of the Ulster Museum gave unstintingly of their advice and knowledge, we are particularly grateful to Dr Bill Maguire, whose words of wisdom informed much of the text and whose published works on Belfast provided crucial references, and to Robert Heslip, Tom Wylie, Pauline Dickson and Richard Warner for the points of specific information, location and interpretation which they supplied with their usual generosity and good humour. We are also grateful for the advice of our colleagues in the Art Department, Brian Kennedy, Eileen Black and Martyn Anglesea. The technical skills and remarkable tolerance of Bill Porter, Bryan Rutledge and Michael McKeown, the Museum's photographers, who supplied all the prints to such quality, often at ridiculously short notice, also deserve a special mention. Thanks are also due to Sandra Neill and Pat McLean of the Museum's Marketing Department for their close attention to issues of copyright and contract. Of those from outside the Ulster Museum who were approached for information, we would like especially to mention Terence Bowman, Alan Boyd, Gerry Cleary, Nicola Gordon-Bowe, Fred Heatley and Myrtle Hill.

We are pleased to incorporate in this edition additional information brought to our attention by Dr D. B. McNeill, formerly Chairman of the Board of Trustees of the Ulster Museum, Jane Leonard now of the History Department, Professor Richard Clarke of Belfast City Hospital, Stephen Gregory, Librarian, Union Theological College, Belfast, Pastor Desmond Cartright, Archivist, Donald Gee Research Centre and Jim Robinson. We are grateful to have had the benefit of their expertise.

Responsibility for error or omission continues to rest, of course, with the authors, who would be pleased to receive any further information on the photographs published. Readers may also like to know that the photographic collections of the Ulster Museum may be consulted by appointment with the History Department, and that reproduction prints of most of the images contained therein can be obtained.